Ailene Nou

M Sarki

AILENE NOU © 2017 M S A R K I

PUBLISHED BY THE
ROGUE LITERARY SOCIETY
MELBOURNE, FLORIDA

PRINTED IN THE USA
ALL RIGHTS RESERVED
RLS007
ISBN-13: 978-0692826294
ISBN-10: 0692826297

I. fiction II. monogamy III. cuckoldry
IV. adultery V. infidelity VI. literary criticism
VII. Nude photography VIII. Adam Phillips
IX. Miguel De Cervantes X. Leo Tolstoy
XI. Claire-Louise Bennett XII. Eimear McBride
XIII. D.H. Lawrence XIV. Elfriede Jelinek
XV. Chris Kraus

BOOK DESIGN & LAYOUT
© 2017 ROGUE LITERARY SOCIETY

ALL PHOTOGRAPHS BY M SARKI

DEDICATION

For Beverly Lane

And for those who are sexually liberated,
and for some who accept they are not

Also by M Sarki:

Zimble Zamble Zumble (limited edition, *elimae books* 2000) poetry

Zimble Zamble Zumble (trade edition, Author's Choice Press 2002) poetry

Little War Machine (Ravenna Press 2004) poetry

Mewl House (Rogue Literary Society 2005) poetry

Any Fucking Day (Rogue Literary Society 2009) poetry

Diary of the Modern God (Rogue Literary Society 2009)

Photographs: People, Places, and Nudes (Rogue Literary Society 2009)

Triple No. 2: No Entry (Ravenna Press 2012) poetry

Shorter Prose (Rogue Literary Society 2013)

Stamped Against the Night (Rogue Literary Society 2014)

Material to Destroy (Rogue Literary Society 2014)

No Entry (Rogue Literary Society 2014) poetry

Table of Contents

Ailene Nou

...it is the obstacle that makes possible the object, that makes possible the idea of someone else...I know what something or someone is by finding out what comes between us.

_____Adam Phillips from *Looking at Obstacles*

If I knew you better I would not be telling you
this. But given you are newly married it is
possible you might derive some benefit from
hearing the sordid details. But you must
promise not to tell anyone. You hear me? I am
afraid hardly one person would understand.
They, at the very least, would judge me or act
horrified by what I did. It is convenient to
condemn people. Believe me, I did not go into
this willy nilly. And please note it was my
husband himself who encouraged me for years
to have an affair, I mean really. And since my
only one close episode was with a principal of
mine back when I still taught grade school in
the summer, I have pretty much let all his
incessant suggesting become simply noise and
static to me. However, his prodding never
ends. But, as you heard me somewhat confess,
something obviously did happen and there is no

explaining away my behavior. I know you haven't known me for long, but can you see me alone in a bar? I have never in my life gone to a place like that by myself, and rarely have I ever been in one. Those places disgust me. But there I was, sitting on a barstool. What possessed me to enter that raunchy old dungeon still confounds my better judgment. But I did, and there is nothing I can do about it now. I am hoping my husband forgives me, but of course he was fiercely agitated over what occurred several years ago with my principal, though he did take full responsibility for its happening afterwards.

You might think my husband and I are crazy but I can't tell you the number of nude photograph sessions we've done, and in places so frightening now to think of them I shudder at the possible consequences had we ever been caught. I have taken my clothes off in downtown Louisville. In some of the worst parts of town, and many times. In fact I have been naked in Cave Hill Cemetery. I have been nude in Black Acre Forest, and it is funny because my old school system owns and manages that property and farm. For several summers now I've gotten naked at the Tawas Point beach in northern Michigan, swam without my suit in Lake Huron, and often strolled without a stitch along the ski trails carved out of the Huron National Forest. I've had my photograph taken with no clothes on at the bottom of Iargo Springs. Frank has photographed me naked at several locations on the high banks overlooking the Ausable River. I have even modeled nude for him in the panhandle of Florida all over the tiny fishing town of Apalachicola. The foliage there alone suggests eroticism. The Spanish moss and live oaks, the swaying palms and wild animals, and so many different varieties of plants it makes you want to do things you only fantasize about.

But we began our nude photography sessions too late. I was already forty years old, but we did our best at making up for lost time. Our plan was to continue on and keep recording my body as I aged, but lately we haven't done much of that. But it hasn't stopped Frank from continuing to imagine me being with other men.

...*The defilement of so sacred and beautiful a thing as marriage is surely the darkest evil that can come to a life....And so I want a fascinating wicked man to come and make me positively, rather than negatively, wicked.*"
___ Mary MacLane from *I Await the Devil's Coming*

All along Frank's idea was for us to do this adultery thing together. And he worried I suppose, and now appropriately, given what I've just done again, that I might take unacceptable measures if left to my own devices. He always insists on collaborating in any deviance that by chance I might become interested in. Or, at the least, he requests he be kept abreast regarding any transgression I am thinking about creating. But rarely, if ever, do I behave as he wants. And not because I am contrary, or as he likes to call me, *insubordinate*. And he knows I am not the sort of person who sits around thinking about fucking somebody other than him. I've never been the type to flirt or dress provocatively. I have always been reserved. How could I be otherwise? My father raised me. And it is Frank who is solely the one to blame for my even considering any adulterous behavior. Of course, part of me at times does want to be a bit naughty, but really, I am satisfied with doing that only with my husband. Why he occasionally wants me with other men I can never quite figure out except that he enjoys my being desired by others. Frank likes that I am attractive, and he encourages me always to feel and look sexy. I do like that about him, but I really do not want to draw attention to myself if I can't do it naturally. I love beautiful clothes, as you know. Just take a look in my closet. But I am very uncomfortable wearing clothes, for example, in which my nipples show through. I don't want anyone feeling uncomfortable because of me. Plus, I do not want to give the wrong impression. But I should be able to wear whatever I want. I am sixty-two years old! And though I do admit to looking pretty damn good for my age, I can't imagine anyone being interested in a woman who is sixty-two. Of course, Frank tells me there are numerous men who would want to have sex with me, who would find me attractive, but that is an idea he obviously covets and what keeps him interested. At least that is what I believe.

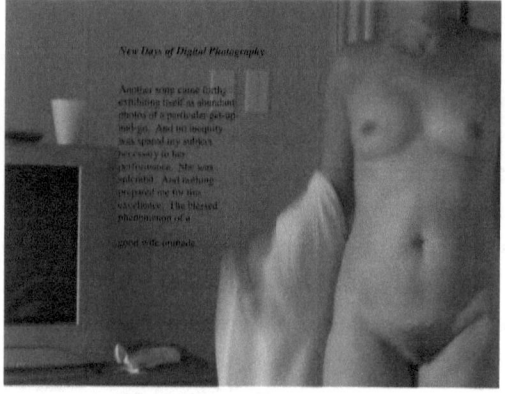

Late season fruits.
The blood orange has its admirer, who suck it smugly.
Cooks stalk it; they'd like to put it in some tartare
sauce. However, some, like me, turn their noses up. In
silence they mould bits of bread into balls, delighting in
their work, then chuck them in God's face.
___Claude Cahun from *Disavowals*

This entire incident in the bar took me by surprise, and I can assure you I won't be doing it again. There I was sitting on a stool, facing the bartender, holding a frilly drink that for some reason I ordered. Even before I finished the silly concoction a man I'd never seen before sidled up to me, and before saying anything, abruptly placed his hand between my legs. Nobody has ever done that, not even in high school and certainly never during my college years. Frank has never been that type of man either. And I don't think it really had anything to do with my being in that seedy bar. This was going to happen no matter where I perched. There have been far too many instances of our talking about this, Frank telling me his plans for some elaborate adultery. And the fact that none of these plans ever came to any fruition make additional suggestions of adulterous behavior seem unreasonable if they are to simply continue on without legs and not require an ending. Fact is, for some reason this particular day I had reached the end of my line with all his talk about me having sex with strangers. Feeling irritably angst I was ready to cross over. So there I was with this man working his fingers between my legs and slipping first one and then another into my vagina. I am fixed on the barstool in shock, but astounded still by the unexpected excitement between my legs, and I suppose I exhibited a bit of fear. Nonetheless, I was completely wet down there and I knew this guy could not be stopped. And I remember my pussy actually dredging itself into his fingers, what Catherine Millet describes as *a baby bird's tirelessly gaping beak*. Here I was stretching my own little beak and hoping for whatever he had to fill it with. But suddenly guilt struck. I had managed again to veer off from our agreed-on collusion. Immediately I realized I had failed for the second time now in not including Frank in my adulterous activities. This epiphany jarred me out of my sexual delirium. I abruptly brushed this stranger's hand away from my genitals and gathered myself enough to quickly exit that dreadful place. I was horrified by what I had done. And embarrassed for what Frank would most likely say to me this time. But, in the same instant, I was mad as hell at him for what he had led me into. This occasion of me sitting alone in a shitty bar with a stranger's dirty fingers shoved up my vagina would never have happened without Frank suggesting it, all his prodding and incessant, nearly daily talk about me having a sexual affair. It wears on a person. But I love him and would do almost anything if he asked me nicely. And I wanted to, and again tried too hard to do it my own way.

We only really value a relationship when it survives our best attempts to destroy it. As every sado-masochist knows, nothing is more seductive than resilience. It is the only aphrodisiac that continues to work the more you

take it. So the only way we can test our infidelity is
through monogamy. A lot of confusion is created by our
belief that it is the other way around.. ___Adam
Phillips from *Monogamy*

Maybe there was part of me who did want to
have that experience. Growing up in a
Lutheran home with four sisters, and having to
attend a Lutheran school my first eight years
would confuse anybody. I finally escaped that
awful experience when the county built a new
public school near our neighborhood. But I am
afraid the Lutherans have permanently damaged
me. All my life I have never known what is
normal. Frank believes, and has been told, that
his sexual fantasy is something every man
secretly wants. He says he has also read enough

about it now to know it's true His problem, he says, is the going through with it. He was raised Lutheran as well. Hard to get past that religion thing and into a healthy sex life after all that guilt and shame gets seared into you. Probably a reason people make some awful mistakes. Like my surprising behavior being more a reaction than a thought-out plan. But Frank insists on us always thinking things through, following each sexual fantasy to its conclusion. And that is where the fantasies always end, the last chapter, the final event. The few times I thought I might be finally prepared to actually do it he ends it as he, to this point anyway, cannot bring himself to allowing another man's penis inside me. And as much as he does imagine me being fucked by somebody other than himself, he cannot bring himself to making it happen. But why does he insist on continually discussing the idea? I wish he would stop all this nonsense. It is confusing for me.

A couple is a conspiracy in search of a crime. Sex is often the closest they can get. ___Adam Phillips from *Monogamy*

Yesterday, Frank was explaining to me about
his paintings. We were on the beach at Avenue
B and I brought up the idea of my talking to
June about showing some of his art in her
gallery. Frank asked why I was suddenly okay
with having artistic expressions of my naked
body displayed publicly when I haven't ever
been agreeable to the idea in the past? I told
him that June's shop just seems the right place
for me to be nude. A lot of women shop at her
store and I know they like beautiful things. I
think there are a lot of women who would want
a beautiful nude painting of a woman hanging
on their wall. Frank was amenable to the idea,
but then he went on about how when he paints
he is basically trying to get as far inside me as he
can. Something about his brush and choice of
color, his strokes and efforts to penetrate. He
says he wants the painting to breathe and come
alive, to which he added that what is presented

as good art around here does not accomplish.
I think his art is good. And I want it shown. I
want to have my naked figure on those walls.
But I don't need to have sex with somebody
other than my husband. Just knowing perhaps
that others find me attractive, or they love my
style, is more than enough for me.

A couple days ago we had to go shopping for a
new countertop for the kitchen and then to
Home Depot so Frank could buy some

fasteners and a few tools he needed to build our new kitchen cabinets. A while back I had decided I was going to wear what I wanted from now on, so I slipped on my old canvass riding leggings I purchased up in Mount Dora at their fantastic annual flea market they call an *Extravaganza.* To these canvas leggings I added a pretty cotton blouse that I left halfway unbuttoned. And as I told you earlier I have decided of late not to wear any bras while living in Florida. I got more than a few looks, and it made me feel good to have the courage to be myself. Frank always encourages me to wear whatever I want. He says he is proud of me and has no problem with anybody enjoying what they see. I am going to do more of that, and it keeps me busy looking for new things for my wardrobe and how to put them all together. For years he has encouraged me to leave my bras at home and to not cover up so much. And feeling sexy is enough for me. I really don't need men hitting on me.

Sometimes I think the attention given to me is really all Frank wants. For a time he searched for a friend he could be intimate with enough that he might share me. But that never happened either. Howard was the only one he ever truly and seriously considered, and even that eventually fizzled out because of Howard's advancing age. He was Frank's teacher and editor, and they became friends. Every year we would go to New York and while there we made a point to visit him, have lunch together, or attend one thing or another. For a time I admit I was interested in pursuing Howard's attention. He was quite the ladies man and part of me wanted to be one of his *concubines*, as he called them. Our affair lasted years but it never ended up with us in bed together. Close, but it never happened. It is a long story and one I am sure Frank will expound on at some point in his writing. Frank certainly expended a great deal of energy pursuing that particular idea. And it enticed him to create many poems dealing with adulterous or salacious behavior. It is surprising to both of us that his poems have not been more recognized. Perhaps some day. History will decide. But for now I must prepare myself to go home and tell Frank what I did. This is not going to be easy. It even disgusts me, the thought of that man's dirty fingers inside me. I just can't explain it. All of a sudden I am entering a darkened bar and ordering a drink, and next thing I know a stranger's claws are working their way into my pussy. How absurd is that? I must have been temporarily insane. Years go by with me acting as the person I think I am and then in an instant I change, or allow myself to assume this other identity that is so foreign in respect to who I believe I am. It is as if I become animal and my lower state, at least the one between my legs, takes over. I suppose if I did google it I too would find it not so abnormal, but it certainly frightens me. I have always equated sex with love, and Frank is the opposite. I know he loves me, adores me even, but he claims never to have had sex for love. He says he fucks me out of lust and purely the pleasure of enjoying my body and what it does for him. Frank insists I have missed too much in my belief there must be love in order to have sex. But then, he does admit that he has never been loved as I have.

I grew up being loved by my father. I knew I was loved. But Frank claims I am the only one who has ever really loved him. And he says he knew that I loved him all those many years ago when we first met, even though it took me an additional twelve years to realize it. To this day Frank feels he lost those years. And during that time he claims he attempted to love others, but found he could not. I ruined him, he says. And he thinks perhaps those lost twelve years is why he never fucks for love. But he tells me often that his greatest satisfaction rests in his gratitude now for having a partner he both loves and lusts. He says when he is in me he cannot help thinking others should be too. That what he has all for himself is in a way criminal, and my pussy should be had by everyone. Frank flatters me by calling my ass *Grade A*. I appreciate his desire for me. And I suppose all his talk and fantasies of me being with somebody other than him ignites his lustful interest in me, and so I collaborate in his fantasies as much as I can.

The fact that jealousy sustains desire—or at least kindles it—suggests how precarious desire is. Not only do we need to find a partner, we also need to find a rival. And not only do we have to tell them apart, we also have to keep them apart. We need our rivals to tell us who our partners are. We need our partners to help us find rivals. ____Adam Phillips from *Monogamy*

I admit we have considered together any number of men. Always Frank's idea mind you, but he gets me involved. How could anyone expect me to escape these thoughts when they are constantly being prosecuted? And they come from every direction. A few years after the event with my principal it was our mailman. Vinnie delivered our mail for nine years. He was the best we ever had. So professional, polite, funny, and handsome. Vinnie was an athlete and had the body of an NBA shooting guard. He was a black man at least ten or fifteen years younger than we were, and very good looking. He had the most engaging personality, and Vinnie and Frank hit it off. Frank would tell me how they chatted about basketball, women and porn, and Vinnie's numerous sexual escapades. He was divorced and lived with the mother of his youngest child, a boy, and this boy was himself a basketball prodigy. Vinnie was so proud of his son, and proud also of his smart oldest daughter from his first marriage who had already finished law school and was well on her way toward accomplishing her goals in life. But Vinnie was a career mailman for the United States Postal Service. He was counting down the years until he could retire. Meanwhile he collected porn dvd's and had as much sex outside his current relationship as possible. Frank told me Vinnie said he drank milk to enrich his erections, and loved to relate his sexual adventures. Frank, as well, loved hearing these tales, and then enjoyed repeating them to me. One of Vinnie's co-workers even told Frank that Vinnie occasionally performed at women's private parties as a male stripper. We weren't surprised, and both of us figured Vinnie was having sex with most of the available women on his mail route, that is, all except me. Really, no woman could possibly resist an advance if he ever made one. And I knew Vinnie liked me. But he claimed to Frank that he never had sex with any woman on his route because it would be a very stupid thing to do and he could lose his job. Frank wanted to believe him, but figured his answer required it be the one he gave regardless of the truth in the matter.

Frank often, throughout the nine years we lived in that house, and unaware of by me, imagined inviting Vinnie over to fuck me. He felt they were pals and Vinnie would appreciate me. Once during a drifting snowstorm Frank even drove Vinnie's stuck little white mail truck out of our unplowed road for him. But as much as Frank liked Vinnie he questioned how much of his desire for Vinnie to fuck me was based on race? He also worried that perhaps Vinnie didn't like him as much as he thought he did. According to Vinnie there were a number of women he was having sex with, and that created a problem when we considered the sexually transmitted diseases he might bring with him into our marital bed. But I liked Vinnie. And with all this talk I did become interested. So much so that when I was alone at home, and Vinnie knocked on the door to personally deliver a package, I became so self-conscious of my strong feelings for him that it made me frightened and nervous and I would quickly get rid of him. But when I was outside weeding our flower beds, Vinnie would stop on his route to flirt with me, and I enjoyed flirting back, something I rarely did.

...Women have gone to the negro for sexual power because of the degeneration of the white man, but there was more than that which impelled her: the negro's primitivism was the same as hers; the language of the emotions, lost to man (having become the capitalist, the analyst, the man of science), was the same...The problem of primitive races is in great closeness to the revolution of women. ___Anaïs Nin, *Mirages, The Unexpurgated Diary of* Anaïs Nin 1939-1947

When my older sister came from out of town to visit us she would leave notes for Vinnie outside our front door, and sometimes from Florida she would mail us letters with personal notes written on the envelope for Vinnie to see. A couple years after she left and returned home Frank asked Vinnie if given the chance would he have fucked his sister-in-law? His eyes immediately lit up and Vinnie answered *Yes!* Frank told me just this morning that after we moved downtown he occasionally saw Vinnie, waved to him from the car, and Vinnie was always friendly as can be, still delivering mail in our old neighborhood. Because of Vinnie's excitement over my sister, Frank told me he has always wanted to stop and ask Vinnie if he would have fucked me had he arranged for it to happen back when we still lived in the neighborhood. And I responded with, *Why don't you ask him?* Of course Frank did not follow through, and nothing ever became of any of these seductions either. But a stupid thing like this bar scene occurs and here I am faced with having to explain again a bad behavior. But Frank will most likely forgive me, just as he has in the past. And at least I did not let that filthy scene go any further, or progress into something I would really be distraught over and ashamed of. I swear I was temporarily insane. But I am afraid no one would ever believe me except Frank.

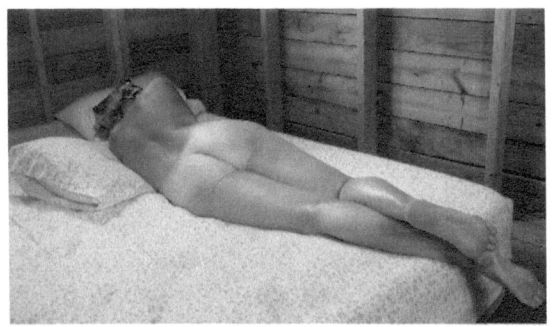

All my life I have ultimately been the guilty one in anything bad involving me. Or at least I am the one who is blamed. Frank thinks it is because I fail to think things through, to see the big picture. But maybe I can't ever see the big picture? For years I heard him instruct our young son to *don't get caught in the wave*. I guess Frank figured our boy got a little of that from me and was worried about him. Or maybe Frank had his own experiences dealing with it. Frank does insist the few occasions he used LSD as a young man helped him see things differently. He says when he needs to he can still get outside himself, and from that lofty distance objectively observe his own behavior. But not always. When he is angry he sometimes goes off the deep end and his emotions take over. But those times when he is in control, and being rational and steady in his reasoning, he claims he can get outside himself. I admit to not knowing how to do that. Like extracting your consciousness from your body. I can't imagine myself in that state, and I never did

LSD. The concept seems quite strange to me. Not sure if I even believe him, but I have heard it explained by others the same way so Frank might know what he is talking about. Anyway, we all have our particular eccentricities. Mine are *pretty things*. Beautiful really. I love beautiful things and want to own them. Old mostly, and not junk like Frank calls them, but pieces nobody can make anymore. Or at least appreciate like I do. I spend hours searching for these treasures. I can get lost in my seeking, my eyes glistening over with excitement in the chase. My slow meandering through small shops and antique malls, making sure not to miss anything, probably spending far too great a time for what I end up achieving. But I don't care. It is what I do. I would rather spend my days looking for treasure then half the things Frank spends his time doing. And mostly it has to do with me. He is obsessed with me and I am flattered, but there seems so much more to life than being immersed in some sexual fantasy. He swears it is better than the so-called *real world*. Frank insists he would rather live in this virtual world he has created than the one he was born into. And who am I to decide what is best for him? We all get to make our own way. Our individual mistakes are most likely numerous, but certainly not unique. But one error in judgment can ruin us forever. The only mistakes worth making are those that can be corrected. There has to be a way out or the adventure can be deadly. And that is why we eventually get stopped in our adulterous tracks and lose our will to proceed. The path becomes too dangerous and the results too final. Better to briefly sample the danger and not perform the final act.

I guess my bar scene was both a tasting of iniquity and my unwillingness for it to go any further. Maybe what I end up describing to Frank will be acceptable to him and perceived as me actually taking the initiative to experiment a little before making a much larger mistake. How could I have known I would enter that darkened place had I not spontaneously just gone ahead with it? It is possible, although improbable, that Frank will be proud of me, just as he eventually was over my now-ancient principal story. I have never told anyone about this man and what I did, but it certainly resulted in one very close call.

Monogamy and infidelity: the difference between making a promise and being promising. ___Adam Phillips from *Monogamy*

Several years ago Frank began encouraging me to stray outside our marriage. And this fantasy of his went on for months. By this time it was summer again, and instead of enjoying my break from teaching, I decided we needed extra money. And for several years I had continued to work over the summer instead of enjoying my time off swimming and hanging around the pool. My parents had retired and moved to Florida and their pool was no longer an option, but still, summer brings on such a sensuous feeling. Summer is sexy, and with Frank planting salacious ideas and constantly talking about them I am not surprised I found myself falling for this man I was working for. In many ways my principal reminded me of Frank. His wife had been sick for some time and she wasn't going to get any better. I can't remember what disease she had, but whatever it was made having sex impossible for them. I felt sorry for Bill. That was his name. Same name as my dad too, which also had something to do with my falling for him. He felt safe to me, and I was certain he would appreciate my body. Our affair began innocently enough. A little flirting, us talking on a few occasions, getting to know each other. Mostly me asking him questions and listening to him. Bill was smart and charming. It was obvious soon enough that we were both interested in each other. I let him know I was available even though he knew I was married. I never once told him anything about Frank, and I should have, but I was not used to conducting an infidelity and had no idea how to proceed. I just don't think like Frank does. I go by feeling. I had simply decided this was going to be the man I would choose to complete what I considered to be my assignment. But I got lost in the fever of it all. I failed to inform Frank about my activities. One thing led to another and here I was suddenly in my principal's office seducing him after a day's work while he talked on the phone. There was nothing he could do about me standing behind his chair, pressing one of my breasts into his shoulder and then against his ear, slipping a photograph onto his desk showing me in the hospital years ago breastfeeding my baby. It was the only picture I had at the time showing me at all naked. My bare breast bursting and my baby latched onto it. Kind of silly now looking back that I would consider that picture sexy enough to turn a man on. But I did, and like I said, it was the only picture I had to excite him and project what I intended him to have. Problem was his secretary was in the very next room. There was only a closed door separating us, and she could have walked in at any time. And had she, I suppose we both could have been fired. And that would have just been my luck. But I decided to leave his office and come directly home to tell Frank what I was intending to do with my principal. And did Frank ever blow.

It was very confusing to me as I thought I was

doing what he wanted me to do. I was so
embarrassed. Frank has a tendency to scold me
when he is angry. I understand now the way I
went about it was the wrong way, and he did
forgive me and take full responsibility for what
happened, but it was a nasty incident that
needed time and more discussion for us to get
through. And we have talked about it a lot
actually. He is sorry for the way he initially
handled my announcement to him. My guess is
he got scared. He wasn't expecting I might on
my own do such a thing, and it caught him off
guard. I felt bad about it for a very long time.
And the rest of that summer, working there for
the principal, was pure misery. Bill would not
let go his interest for me. He would email me
often. Finally I told him to never contact me
again. And he honored my request. But just
recently Frank brought up the principal again
and he asked me several questions he needed
answered. I told him everything I could
remember and he remained kind and extremely
interested. He regrets I did not tell him further
about the emails and then running into Bill the
next year. He thinks now how exciting it would
have been to have him over to get to know him.
As far as our collaborating together to find the
right man for me, he believes that this guy was
our best chance for conducting a safe adultery.
But a couple years ago Bill died a of a sudden
heart attack.

...Strangeness is exciting but it threatens to derange us;
routine is comforting but it threatens to put us to sleep...
___Adam Phillips from *Monogamy*

What makes a person so unhappy and
confused? If I knew I would write a book
about it. Probably would still take a lifetime.
And what if I did change? What if everything
finally did become clear to me and I realized life
was all one big joke? That nothing really
mattered anyway. That all we were here for was
to have a good time? But I know truly good
times are hard to come by. And this latest
incident too will pass. Life does have its daily

challenges. No escaping the hard times and getting all bent up over them. But that is easier said than done. And we shall see where my latest escapade takes me. Frank is not going to like that I let a complete stranger put his fingers in my pussy. I know that for a fact. But the truth is he knows it is mine to do with as I please. He has no say in what I put in there. Oh he can get furious and rant and rave about like a madman, but I have the final say. And for thirty-three years I have saved myself for only him. He knows that all too well. And I have never intended for it to be otherwise.

*...How do you know what your desire is? It is that which makes you feel guilty when you betray it; not when you betray someone else, but when you betray yourself; indeed, for Lacan self-betrayal, the self-betrayal of giving up on one's desire, is the source of guilt. We suffer from failures of ruthlessness...___*Adam Phillips from *Missing Out*

This sharing thing is all of Frank's making. But I clearly have my part in it. Why we are not simply satisfied with taking nude photographs of my body and sharing them on the internet is beyond me. We used to have an art blog, a memoir of sorts, anonymous, and we posted nude pictures he took of me. It was fun. And dangerous too. But we always were more than a little concerned that somebody from my school would recognize me and I would get fired from my job. Elementary school teachers are generally not nude art models. Even if you are attempting to make art, nudity is frowned upon. Plus we were seriously writing about adultery and triangles and the idea of possibly sharing me with another man. A pretty sinful premise to some people. But we never actually did anything. It was all just talk and speculation over what would occur, or result, if we did go through with it. For better or worse it is what has kept our marriage interesting. Adultery is no longer a mystery to us. We have played around with the idea of being naughty for a such long time now, and still we have remained monogamous. A bit of danger in a relationship is a good thing. Jeopardy can breed success. The psychoanalyst Adam Phillips says we need to know something about what we don't get, and about the importance of not getting it. And in our almost countless and flawed ways, that is what we're working on.

We may believe in sharing as a virtue—we may teach it to our children—but we don't seem to believe in sharing what we value most, our sexual partners. But if you really loved someone, wouldn't you want to give them the best thing you've got, your partner? It would be a relief not to be puzzled by this. ___Adam Phillips from *Monogamy*

Additional Source Material

Don Quixote, or The Man Who Was Recklessly Curious

... when you can recognize people there's no enchantment at all, just a lot of bruising, and a lot of bad luck.
___Sancho Panza, *Don Quixote*

Miguel De Cervantes was criticized for "interruptions" in the action of his epic novel *Don Quixote* by his use of adding interpolated stories, or novellas. Four hundred years ago he unexpectedly digresses from the main text, disregarding his main character Don Quixote in the chapter *The Impertinently Curious Man,* and presents an adulterous story examining a perfectly happy union between a lucky man and the most beautiful and chaste woman of the country. The married man named Anselmo asks his loyal friend Lotario to seduce his wife Camila in order for them to test her fidelity to him. This particular novella was a retelling of a tale from canto 43 of Ariosto's poem *Orlando furioso* written sometime in the years between 1516 and 1532. The issue of a triangular infidelity among friends being examined by Cervantes over four hundred years ago was somewhat surprising. And though Lotario repeatedly attempts to resist and remain himself chaste, he finally succumbs to Anselmo's threat of ending their long friendship if he refuses to at least attempt this infidelity. Cervantes goes on to detail this elaborate affair of deceit and deception, and refers to these two men as the *reckless man and traitorous friend*. Needless to say, both the infidelity and friendship crumbled. Now guilty of this transgression Lotario safely hides Camila in a convent and flees the country. Repentant, he subsequently dies fighting for the French in a battle not his own. The husband Anselmo takes his own life believing the actual testing of his wife's chastity was both foolish and reckless. And after hearing the dreadful news regarding both her lovers, Anselmo's wife Camila takes vows to live out the rest of her life as a nun in the convent where Lotario had previously hidden her safely from her husband.

Levitating Above the Bane

The Kreutzer Sonata by Leo Tolstoy deals
primarily with the subject of sex and desire.
Books about jealousy and adulterous behavior
always compete for my attention, but I have
never been a fan of Tolstoy. I did read an essay
by J.M. Coetzee where he said *The Kreutzer
Sonata* was one of the three greatest works
written on the subject of male sexual jealousy.
But this Tolstoy novella resulted in
disappointment for me. The abrupt ending was
a bit extreme as determined by the eventual
slaying of the narrator's wife as she was
enjoying a private midnight supper with her
young musician friend while her husband was
supposed to be off far away on a business trip.
And though a bit of urgency was obviously
paramount for a clearer communication among
the three parities involved, I did not believe
their adulterous affair needed to end so
violently.

The narrator of *The Kreutzer Sonata* derived
intense erotic feelings whenever his imagination
reined over his reality. His wife was attractive
and had taken good care of herself, and for that
her husband was eternally grateful. And the
fact that other men found her appealing also
added to his sensual excitement. But because
of his wife's naiveté regarding her own feelings

for becoming an object of desire, her husband ultimately did not trust her and believed she would succumb in time to a fornicator's talented advances. Besides, he knew every ploy of a fornicator as he himself was one. Therefore, he could not trust this newly-smitten musician acquaintance to not betray the sanctity of his marriage, but rather to conquer and bed his wife after gaining her affections. This typical *dance with deceit* that some couples engage in should not have transpired. Feelings could have instead been expressed wholly to each other. However, the jeopardy involved in such honest confessions among couples is too dangerous for most of us, and there is also some masculine resistance for completely baring one's soul.

But beyond this initial fear for naked exposure and embarrassment due to expressing some uncomfortable truth, is the uncertain path to righteousness. It is even possible that the musician would have eventually become the husband's friend and his advances toward intimacy might have naturally developed as imminent. But because of these heartfelt and often frightening discussions between parties, it depends on the bond developed among these new friends as to whether or not anything sexual would come of their plans. If the participants instead found they were basically incompatible, and the musician in fact could not be made the husband's friend, any previous flirtation would resolve itself as inappropriate. This resulting judgment would certainly deem any further engagement between the potential adulterers as unacceptable. But this all should have been established long before the husband left town on business. And his wife and her musician friend should not have been carrying on this secret affair even in light of their seemingly innocent love for playing music together. These two, sharing a late supper together after the children were put to bed, would appear to any jealous, non-communicative husband, as treacherous. And the unhappy result leaves his wife collapsed onto the floor, stabbed in the heart, and bleeding to death.

Depending on Chance

In her short story *Morning, 1908* Claire-Louise
Bennett writes masterly of what it feels like to
find oneself in a potentially compromising
situation and then to realize it may have been
what she wanted in the first place. Wandering
outside on a summer evening in only her
nightgown with a coat thrown over, and
meandering downgrade from her cottage door
to the edge of a fence and gate containing
several grazing cows, the narrator is startled to
see a young man with a backpack making his
way up the remote road towards her. She is
immediately taken by fear that he has eyed her
and that it is she he comes for. After
considering the consequences of possibly being
raped she decides it might actually not be the
worst outcome for her, almost recreational, and
something dogs routinely do. It occurs to her
that it may be possible that this young man is
what she wants anyway, and she well-suited for
the adventure just as she dreamily entered into
her present situation dressed, in her eyes,
almost naked. She knew the stupid overcoat
would offer little protection for her. But every
forward movement the young man proves to
make, as a result, keeps himself a certain
distance from her, and finally her squandered
imagination for a sexual fantasy is all that
remains.

Just for a moment everything gathered in dreadful
suspension, my eyes gaped, cold and enormous — and
then it all glided backwards into an atmosphere of
broadening redundancy, intersected by a vertical and
rather searing sense of abnegation. And then Bennett
adds, *Remote sensations really, hardly mine at all —*
nothing to take personally.

A Sense of Impossible Excess

Not long after beginning to read *The Lesser Bohemians* by Eimear McBride I questioned why I was engaged in what appeared to be a young woman's coming-of-age story? Of course, the agonist responsible for providing the necessary tension to the female main character of the book is a man twenty years her senior. Their sexual exploits, though non-graphic compared to general fare, were tantalizing due to her offering her naive virginity to him, and then she returning repeatedly to his shabby apartment for more rough and tumble sex until she is forced to deal with the famous actor's unprotected disregard as he irresponsibly ejaculates inside her.

In her novel Eimear McBride expounds on the protagonist's discovery of sex and her infatuation for an older man. Throughout the book the young drama student remains attracted to this older gentlemen for reasons unexplained, and is at first blissfully unaware of him being a famous actor. She simply likes this older man and perhaps believes she can safely learn about sex from him. As the story progresses it is understood he is quite the womanizer, has been previously married, and has a child he does not see or support. He basically lives in a dump, has few possessions other than his acting craft. Hard drink and having sex with licentious women seems to be his primary focus.

While being subjected to McBride's relentless onslaught of abruptly hard language, often in one-word sentences, my mind at times wandered over to consider the obscene numbers of purported May-September trysts engaged in by two of my favorite celebrities, Bob Dylan and Gordon Lish. And parallel to the subject of this novel, little to nothing is ever mentioned in passing, or published in the abundant online mags, about women stating publicly their horror or disappointment in having had sex with these two celebrity provocateurs. Seems the only women who do complain about being made a sexual object or victimized by these two old men are the ones they decide not to bed. Just recently I was relating to my wife the reported liaisons and sexual conquests of Bob Dylan who is described as *a buck in heat during rutting season* in the latest biography I recently reviewed titled *Dylan: The Biography* by Dennis McDougal. Given Dylan's reported bad teeth and reputation for flight I wondered out loud to my spouse my question as to why these women allow Dylan to have his way with them? Her answer was simple, and direct, *Because he's Bob Dylan.* But then, my wife's remark did little to settle my uneasiness over what was proceeding in the pages of *The Lesser Bohemians*. The senior actor in this story has no money to speak of, hauls around an enormous amount of personal baggage, and obviously has deeply ingrained flaws in his character. And even if the young female drama student is using him as mentor it seems she is heading down a path that would certainly lead to eventual destruction.

... To the street where I was before I became what I've become — a form of a thing.

The young lady, in my mind, deteriorates into a somewhat addictive character, hell-bent on destroying herself, or die trying. She throws caution to the wind as she is often inebriated and agreeable to almost anyone having sex with her. It is as if she is punishing herself and her senior lover for their not being fully committed to each other. The actor-with-flaws does attempt to guide the young lady down a more meaningful path, but it is obvious he has developed a relationship not in his best interests. His conquest and spoils prove to be not at all stable.

... I know all about having a good time. Having it and having it until a good time's all there is, until it's not a good time, until it's everything turned to shit and you can't believe the things you've done, look at me, is that what you want?

Eimear McBride writes in a manner not easily understood, but accessible, nonetheless. In staying the course the trampling cadence of her language eventually becomes discernible as meaningful rhetoric. Feeling and emotion within her text quickly becomes physical rather than an initial reliance only on intuition.

Starched and parched I hit in the wings.

Midway through the book there is quite an amazing chapter where it closes with the two age-fated lovers having sex in his pathetic room, an older picture of his daughter propped above them on the bedside table, the photograph depicting a girl who is now about the same age as she is now, and the protagonist admitting to herself that this man whom she is fucking is also a bit like a father to her as well. But the main difference being, she silently tells the photograph as she bites his neck and continues her intercourse, is that *this girl cannot make love to her father as I can. And I am his daughter too.*

Gradually her lover offers up his account of growing up in a sexually abusive broken home, detailing his own mother joining the young fourteen year-old boy in bed and touching him inappropriately, enough to make him hard and then come. Several pages of the actor's relating of his mother's incestual advances carry on until the boy reaches the age of sixteen when he finally breaks free from her. But not really. How could he? His life will remain unsettled for eternity, a learned behavior making of him a perpetual vagabond, a man rambling on like a pain locomotive. McBride's language also digresses into the realm of the conventional. No longer the rat tat tat of two-word sentences and shorthand composition as the actor recounts his entire life from the point of escaping his mother until the present.

Interesting how McBride uses a form of shorthand to further the action in this remarkable novel, but when it comes to the protagonist's older actor boyfriend her writing turns conventional perhaps in order for us to understand every important word describing his life, previous and present. The relationship from the beginning portends trouble, and when we learn the young protagonist's name is Eily the reader is exposed to a sympathy mounting for the resulting victim she is certain to become. In now knowing her name the novel becomes personal and there is an emotional connectedness to the young novice. There is a diseased enmeshment between these characters caught in the dark grime of a dirty London. Living adventurously and always wanting more. Impossible results retracted by the wicked. And a flame that seems to never go out.

I'll Kill My Dog Myself

...If you see the point of the great old commandment know thyself, then you see the point of all art.
____D.H. Lawrence from an essay in *Adelphi*

Unfortunately, and contrary to the ideas presented by Geoff Dyer in his book *Out of Sheer Rage: Wrestling With D.H. Lawrence*, I believe the answers to the enigmas of D.H. Lawrence will be found in his fiction rather than in biography or his nonfiction works. Certainly fiction is where he would have wrestled with his demons, provided he had not yet the answers his heart was demanding of him. Nonetheless, *D.H. Lawrence* by Brenda Maddox is a well-written and thoroughly researched biography that offers many theories to ponder regarding several aspects of the Lawrence character.

In this engaging book, Brenda Maddox has presented every fact she could unearth on the sexual enigma of this most-famous and notorious English writer of the Twentieth century. And because of them she offers her own ideas regarding the Lawrence marriage. It was obvious to me that Ms. Maddox attempted to be fair and would even come to the defense of Lawrence regarding some of the mean-spirited and unfair criticism offered on behalf of feminists over the last fifty years or more.

Granted, Lawrence was awful at times, he certainly was opinionated, but Lawrence appears quite fair in his assessments of both men and women. He either liked them or he did not. His severely high and tyrannical standards included an honesty and consistent behavior required of all his acquaintances and especially those he called his friends. Lawrence treated each gender with the utmost respect, liking more the opposite sex, but wishing to acquire deeper physical and emotional relationships with males than were possible in his lifetime. From early on a given fact of life to Lawrence was that women held the ultimate power, and little changed to alter that belief by the time he succumbed to lung disease at the age of forty-four years.

Brenda Maddox entertained the idea that Lawrence was conflicted in his ideas and feelings regarding the male sex. She reported at least one incident of homosexual love and surmised there may have been others. But her main premise was that Lawrence perhaps searched his whole life for a bisexual male lover and never found the right match. A theory such as this compounds the answers and results in a more specific question as to why? It is possible that too much attention has been placed on the homoerotic Lawrence and not enough on his burning desire to please sexually, once and for all, his beloved, and one-abiding-love, Frieda.

In his time, Lawrence was creating erotic heterosexual fiction of the first rank, enough to have him crucified and burned at the stake if it were even remotely possible for such a judgment to be issued. He did with coitus what none other before him had accomplished on the page. He was accused of being a pornographer due to his infamous novel *Lady Chatterley's Lover.*

One serious problem in this biography was the preoccupation Maddox herself had on sodomy. For whatever reason, Maddox had a personal fixation on the anus in as much as she reported and offered proof of the couple repeating the one sexual act binding the two lovers together as deemed "special" and "separate" from all others in the totality of their affairs. The fact that this special privilege between them was not only unlawful, but an even unspeakable act, may have held great interest for both of them. And the possible homoerotic suppression of his own tendencies toward loving sexually a person of his own sex, and his hatred or inadequacy present in his quest for supremacy over the women in his life may or may not have contributed to his surly and disagreeable behavior at times. Lawrence obviously had ideas and fantasies he ultimately did suppress from Frieda, but only because he could not discover ways in which to manifest them in their lives. He, I suppose as most of us do, took his failures out on the closest person to him, that being Frieda, and was also, perhaps as a consequence of his bad behavior, still very loving and grateful, needing her almost-constant presence in his life most of the time.

Maddox is careful not to brand Lawrence a homosexual, but she does go to some length in advancing her theory of suppressed feelings of Lawrence for persons of his own sex and the trouble it caused him in his relationships with women. At any rate, if true, it allowed for his readers a smorgasbord of sexual and sensual delight. It is somewhat surprising to me that after his death friends and associates disclosed various endeavors made throughout his entire life in his search for a bisexual partner. I am not sure if this means that Lawrence desired the same male lover for himself to join in the conjugal affairs with his wife Frieda.

Throughout their long relationship, almost from the very beginning, it is widely documented that Frieda had affairs with countless other men. Whether these affairs were meant to punish Lawrence for his extreme or controlling behavior, or to teach him more about the liberating effects of sexual freedom, Frieda was most certainly the one in charge of their sex life. There was nothing Lawrence could do to stop her sexual promiscuity and Brenda Maddox dutifully reports that he skillfully and wisely used her experiences and tales of sexual freedom in the many characters present in his novels and short stories. And that is where I think the other revealing truths just might be found. It is my somewhat outlandish premise that Lawrence too was looking to share his marriage bed, but with a man he loved as much as he did himself, a man he could not himself have sex with but embrace and hold as partners in love, both sexually loving the same beautiful, free, and voluptuous woman in the wide-open presence and nakedness of each other. An often ravaging sexual caress together consummated by two great friends both day and night, always culminating with the ascendant and esteemed Frieda. But that man never did exist for Lawrence, and it is quite possible he could not have exacted either love, even as much and as hard as he may have diligently searched and desired for them.

Behind the Cross Lurks the Devil

Elfriede Jelinek is a poet. Or her translator,
Michael Hulse, is a poet. It matters not to me
who the responsible party is here. Fact is,
Jelinek's novel *Lust* is a masterpiece in brutal
honesty. Fiction as fact. I know these people
she writes about and they exist in the world I
live in. They always have. They are my
neighbors and we live in the same town.

A third of the way into this beautifully
profound, though vicious treatise, the narrator,
after somewhat sarcastically speaking of a
factory worker fetching from the dispenser a
refreshing Coke, says the word *I*. She, or he,
unhesitatingly and frankly makes strong claims.

Wood is pulped and the pulp is processed at the mill by
people who've been pulped...

Obviously the opinions voiced in this narrator's
countless personal attacks are broad and
thoroughly encompassing. Because of
mounting evidence and personal experience I
feel confident that Elfriede is not exclusively a
man-hater as others have previously suggested.
To label her one is totally unfair. Obviously she
equally hates all that is oppressive and insanely
preposterous, which covers enormous swaths
of ground and leaves her much else to expose in

the course of her saying so. As for the pitiful women she portrays in her books she clearly positions herself above and beyond them, and in fact holds the women responsible for the spousal abuse they receive inasmuch as they are themselves slaves to wanting the things and prestige that only money can buy. This mass disease of consumerism is as much at fault as the worldly desire for more money and property. Through the ages this hunger has undoubtedly proven to feed a vicious cycle of abuse. In matters of sexual behaviors Jelinek goes well over the line in order to be herself appropriately absurd. The gargantuan number of orifices filled and splayed seem almost hilarious and often delightfully insane.

...Nature presupposes sheer scale: anything of a smaller size could never excite us or entice us, tempt us to buy a dirndl dress or a hunting outfit...

She is equally without hope for all who are oppressed. It is our human condition. Oppressed people the world over resort to life's foibles to determine the results and direction of their flawed and blemished lives. The ones-in-charge continue to profit and consider themselves superior in their disgusting delusions of grandeur. There are so many of life's examples to this affect that Jelinek has little trouble digressing and exploring the diverse and meandering avenues and

countrysides of our often pathetic and
meaningless existence.

*...All day long a man lives off the beautiful image of his
wife, only to have her nag all evening...She and the
village women and all of us, there we stand, dripping
and thawing, facing the kitchen stove and counting the
tablespoonfuls in which we dole ourselves out...*

Unrelenting in her assault of all, and the insults
she spews upon us, Jelinek scours her cynical
mind for the strongest corrosive agent she may
engage. Her courageous honesty is so absurd to
be somewhat funny and profanely enjoyable to
read. A weak mind of lesser character could
never delight in these scribblings patterned in
short paragraphs of hers that never fail to
inspire a reader to go on and hear what else she
might have to say about these people we all
should be aware of and know. Otherwise we are
one of them as well. Better to be a recreational
observer slouched within the stuffing of our
leisure chair, devoid of any personal feeling of
responsibility that urges us to also merge within
these irrelevant lives as additional willing
participants.

*...Even the station-master's slender signal baton is
almost too much for her. She is obeying her own
command. And no one else's... In the midst of her life,
this woman often likes to think she has to get out of her
alignment alongside other women with sagging breasts*

and hopes who have docked beside her…

Jelinek, in her way, promotes self-awareness and personal responsibility. When a reader is offended by these painfully direct accounts and graphic details explicitly made out for us, it causes me to pause and consider the source of these complaints. I credit them to an additional version of the typically judgmental and self-righteous ones who hold little to no credibility based on their own typically guilty history. The sensitive man who feels somehow affronted as well is considered in less than a good light. We are all complicit of these same behaviors and thoughts no matter how hard we impress ourselves and others in our attempts to deny them.

For wary readers it seems Jelinek's incessant bombardment is meant to wear one down. She is anything but taciturn in her sometimes disgusting assaults so perversely avowed. Two-thirds through this generous tirade marks a new measure of tiredness. She flirts with boredom. It is possible the book could have ended at this same mark. But perhaps she still has something new and yet unheard of to say? Surely it is hoped her constant fucking and sucking might beget some new meaning. It is true the hairdresser fails at keeping Gerti *fresh*. No longer available to Jelinek are any additional analogies for a subject going downhill.

...The woman doesn't improve from constant use, but if she herself wants to avail herself of a young man, make herself available to a fellow who lives nearby: no, it won't do! ...

So Gerti degrades herself even more. A husband who uses her every orifice to fill and gorge with his own juices and then leaves her soiled and bent with nary a kiss goodbye is still not enough abuse for her so Gerti ventures out to seek more in the shape and forms of youth that are now and forever escaping her.

...But we, us extras, we are so difficult to move, we hang leaden upon our catheters, through which our warm waste waters trickle wretchedly away...

Being drunk and spread out on the snow *of her own digging*, wanting too much to be loved, *enamored of herself*, delusional enough so that gangs of young men and women are allowed to expose and fondle, grab and mishandle her hidden places, her creases and folds torn and spread enough to spew their juices laughably, considered by these kids as no longer needed and instead worn and desperately used up.

...Gerti is put in her car. Quiet, now! How shall I put it? She has been at the mercy of hands and tongues...

And for some of us roughly groped and fondled

like this would be just what we have wanted. An orgy designed for denying personal despair. But not Gerti. She wants the young man Michael and not the rest of what comes with him. The narrator frankly tells us that *this woman has to get attached to an asshole like Michael, of all people… He grabs roughly inside the front of her coat and dress, and, laughing, tugs and twists her nipples…*

The book is strikingly more about regrets over life choices rather than the popular blurbed *war between the sexes*. Poor choices and not being true to one's self plays into this work in far greater measure than feminism and spousal abuse. On almost every page men and women being caught up in superficial looks and pretentious appearances are shown as contagious diseases prevalent throughout our consumer-driven societies.

…Torn and tormented, we become visible, and we want to look good for others, to think of what we paid for our clothes, we no longer have what we paid and we notice the lack when we have to undress and caress our partner in love…

Defeated, in the world of lust, youth rules. Age is not kind, and life simply wears one out.

…Thus their round fat bodies hum away, life goes on, man vanishes continually in death, the hours sink to the ground, but women flit numbly about the house, never

safe from all the blows that fate deals…

And there finally is no hope. Ultimately a god is blamed or held responsible for this creation. It is hard to imagine a work like this becoming popular.

…Flabbergasted, the men gape into their women's holes, torn by life, and yes, they shudder, as if they knew that the box had long been empty from which the seeds have been shaken out for years. But the dear women are so attached to them…

In Search of Our Crime

Art is the consequence of that excess, that energy or force, that puts life at risk for the sake of intensification, for the sake of sensation itself—not simply for pleasure or for sexuality, as psychoanalysis suggests—but for what can be magnified, intensified, for what is more, through which creation, risk, innovation are undertaken for their own sake, for how and what they may intensify.
___Elizabeth Grosz, *Chaos, Territory, Art: Deleuze and the Framing of the Earth* (New York: Columbia University Press, 2008)

Understandably, in the novel *I Love Dick* by Chris Kraus, it seems boredom is the original driving force behind the adulterous fantasy being planned and played out between a married couple. The aging Sylvère is quite a bit older than his wife and for years now their sex life has taken a backseat to their work in academics, film, and the theater. Because of the husband's disinterest in having sex the couple willingly decides to begin plotting a possible ménage à trois. Due to a fortuitous get-together with Sylvère's associate Dick, a collaboration of seduction of the likely candidate evolves that combusts in a rekindling of sexual interest in each other. When the couple themselves are not having sex they spend their time together fervently composing letters and making phone calls to their subject Dick in order to seduce him. This titillating process ignites a new and robust sex life that for years has been absent in their relationship.

... But Dick , I know that as you read this, you'll know these things are true. You understand the game is real, or even better than, reality, and better than is what it's all about. What sex is better than drugs, what art is better than sex? Better than means stepping out into complete intensity...

The novel *I Love Dick* proceeds in corresponding fashion, and through the journaled days their life is examined and digressions made into all facets of their relationship together, always keeping Dick their focus and the prize. A frenzy of activity follows for three days until life's demands and prior commitments portends an unfavorable result and a lessening of expectations. Regardless, the collaborative seduction continues as a private exercise between the couple and a way for them to remain interested in their sexual life together. But as everything else, that exercise as well runs its course and Chris is left to continue her crush and game all by herself.

...Art supersedes what's personal.

My favorite epistolary novel *Epigraph* by Gordon Lish surprisingly fails to show up in the Wikipedia List of contemporary epistolary novels. *I Love Dick* doesn't either, but Kraus mentions Habermas, or perhaps Lukács first, as saying the epistolary genre marked the advent of the bourgeois novel. Epistolary fiction dates back at least to ancient Roman times, but it is said the epistolary novel as a distinct genre first gained prominence in Britain in the mid-eighteenth century. Female characters in these novels often wrestled with sexual temptation and moral propriety and found that the only way to express themselves honestly and thoroughly was by confiding in a trusted friend through letters. Chris Kraus, our main character in *I Love Dick*, writes *Sylvère keeps socializing what I'm going through with you. Labeling it through other people's eyes …This presumes that there's something inherently grotesque, unspeakable, about femaleness, desire.*

Desire plays the most important role. Whether it is its lack or an abundance makes little difference. Chris holds her desire in spades. On the other hand, Sylvère needs an impetus in order to be sexually charged again, so he adds another man into the relationship offering up the possibility for intensity. The idea of a condoned and sanctioned infidelity is generally exciting. And that two male associates would be sharing the same woman offers a potential binding love between these two fellows that could in fact enhance their already homosocial relationship. But does Sylvère have his wife's best interests in mind, or because of his own boredom directs the action of his fantasy?

The initial flirtation occurring between Dick and Chris at dinner was brought up over breakfast the next morning by Chris in order for examination and a search for truth. Because this decade-old couple previous to this affair were no longer having sex with each other they nurtured and kept vital their relationship by telling each other everything, much in the vein of Jean-Paul Sartre and Simone de Beauvoir. Chris informs Sylvère of the previous night's flirtation with Dick as amounting to what she termed a *Conceptual Fuck*. The continued seductive dance, though eventually collaborative, is initiated by Sylvère. And after 180 pages into their undelivered *billets-doux* to Dick the couple decides rather to make art. The altered plan then proceeds with the promise to eventually present their growing number of letters as a performance piece. But unfortunately *I Love Dick* finds itself expanding into an unfeeling academic treatise involving essays that have nothing to do with Dick, but instead demonstrate to the reader how well-informed and intellectual all these special people are, as well as a platform for Kraus and her axe to grind.

… Love and sex both cause mutation, just as I think desire isn't lack, it's surplus energy — a claustrophobia

inside your skin —...

After finally spending four rapturous days and
nights at the home of Dick, Chris is spurned by
her lover with words to the effect of *What did
you expect?* And following this devastatingly long
weekend, after confiding to Sylvère of her
heartbreak and disappointment, his response is
similar to she says a *cut-rate therapist* who
counsels, *You'll never learn...You keep looking for
rejection! It's the same problem that you've always had
with men.*

*... Even though Dick's rejected her, she's managed to
cover all the bases: She doesn't need him to respond for
her love to go on. She can maintain a relationship with
me (*Sylvère*), draw inspiration from Dick for her
work, and even put her film into a vault without using it
even further...*

In the second half of *I Love Dick* the Us vs.
Them battle ripens. Why is it that for some
feminists it has to always be about women
against men? I think it sounds petty to read
Kraus complain that *...while these men were getting
famous...me and all my friends, the girls, were paying
for our rent and shows and exploring "issues of our
sexuality" by shaking to them all night long in topless
bars. ...Why is it men become essentialists, especially in
middle age?*

From the beginning of time those who

considered themselves intellectuals, and members of an elitist group, generally consisted of men. For some radicalized feminists, those organizations have always been unacceptable. But a woman who also wants to be an accepted member of that awful crowd says more than her exclusion from it. Our greatest thinkers and writers of this, or any time, generally avoid being associated with any group, and if a truly great mind finds itself a member of some elitist social group he, or she, tends to eventually escape from it and typically stands alone on a unique difference. A genius speaks for itself, and no exclusionary club is ever promoted on its behalf. It is ludicrous to think that because these stereotypical male intellectuals fiercely protect their sacred clubs and bloated importance, female thinkers of the same ilk form their own groups seemingly in order to do battle with them. And each club's goal seems always to be the most impressive, and the louder their expression the greater the flashing glare. The fact that both groups remain exclusionary and protectively elite says more about them than the complaint raised over sexism. Both are silly, and at fault, in their incessantly foolish chatter. As well as women, countless men too have been excluded from these male intellectual bodies. Why would anyone want to be a member of one of these exclusionary fraternities or sororities anyway?

Genuine thinking is a violent confrontation with reality, an involuntary rupture of established categories.

Chris Kraus has written a most impressive book. But she fails in her somewhat bitter agenda to garner acknowledgment of her own importance. Nonetheless, she is a writer worth reading.

White Tulips in a Vase

There were squirrels or woodchucks, or some
animal or other in the show's title pasted on my
television screen, and the heading had little to
nothing to do with what was to follow. Seems
the wife in the story was required to cheat on
her banker husband and report the act in detail
back to him in order to save her marriage. The
banker, being an admitted masochist, needed to
know for a fact that she was actually going
through with the adultery because, for one
reason or another, he just did not believe she
was actually cheating on him. A bumbling
detective Hank Dolworth is forced to spy on
the banker's wife as requisite in securing a
mortgage for a house Hank wants to buy back
from his ex-wife who he remains in love with
but who is newly engaged to be married. While
tailing the banker's wife, Hank is discovered and
confronted. By enquiring firsthand with the
banker's wife he learns all the sordid details of
their marriage. She confesses to Hank that she
did actually go through with her husband's first
request for infidelity, but after he made
demands on her to continue conducting this
salacious behavior on a regular basis, and then
provide him every detail, she resisted. The
banker's wife claimed she had no interest at all
in continuing to cuckold her husband, but now
she was forced to lie about her required

dalliances, and this present ruse was driving her crazy. She felt compelled to make up stories of transgression even as she dined alone, providing her husband with receipts for lunches that included wine, visits to museums and such, in order to falsely prove to him she was having the sort of date with another man her husband was expecting of her. The most absurd concept of this marriage arrangement was the banker's insistence on divorcing her if she did not comply with his adulterous demands.

Hank, the detective, was astounded and horrified, and could not grasp the fundamental concept of the banker's desire to have his attractive and loyal wife cuckold him. In no uncertain terms Hank expressed to his business partner his consternation that there might be people out there in the world who did this sort of thing. He thought the banker must certainly be crazy, and believed that if anyone else knew about this they would think the banker crazy too. Hank just couldn't get his head around the idea that every man might secretly wish to see his wife with another, and that this sexual fantasy is not at all unusual, nor even the unnatural act Hank has made it out to be. And doubtful any prior consideration was given Hank to the idea that if there was never a threat for losing one's lover to another the mating dance would rarely occur in the first place.

As the storyline progressed, Hank arranges for his business partner to be a make-believe lover to the banker's wife. An adulterous motel date is staged and photographed for the husband to observe for himself the truth of what his wife has been reporting to him all along. And because of the detective's contrived success in proving the banker's cuckolding terms are indeed being satisfied, the detective's loan is secured as well as the marriage relationship saved. But for whatever reason the husband in due time finds he still cannot believe her, and after doing a little internet research of his own regarding the detective, the banker finds Hank's business partner to be a planted adulterer and the entire event exposed as fraudulent. When confronted with this truth the banker's wife confesses, and unknown to Hank his loan approval is suddenly terminated.

Of course, the banker's wife promptly seeks Hank out in order to responsibly inform him of the latest development due to her confession, and then the most unlikely scenario takes place, given what they both had proclaimed earlier, and these two supposedly ethical beings spend the night together in bed. The woodchuck story ends as the banker husband leaps to his death from his high rise window after Hank, in another failed attempt to re-secure his loan, claims and proves to the cuckolded banker that for hours, just the night before, he himself was fucking his cheating wife.

About the author

Besides being an accomplished poet with four collections published, M Sarki travels, writes literary reviews, paints a bit, and occasionally takes a photograph in his attempt to create an artifact. Riding around on his Electra Townie 3-speed, drinking good coffee, and taking long walks on the beach with his wife and dog make for good days. Beverly Lane continues to arouse Sarki's attention; a degree of gaze and obsession that has spanned now for over forty-five years.

M Sarki has written, directed, and produced six short films titled *Gnoman's Bois de Rose*, *Biscuits and Striola*, *The Tools of Migrant Hunters*, *My Father's Kitchen*, *GL*, and *Cropped Out 2010*. He is also the author of the feature film screenplay, *Alphonso Bow*.

www.ingramcontent.com/pod-product-compliance
Lightning Source LLC
Chambersburg PA
CBHW020804130626
46554CB00006B/2309